THE DAY OF THE JACKDAW

Published by Barrington Stoke
An imprint of HarperCollins*Publishers*
Westerhill Road, Bishopbriggs, Glasgow, G64 2QT

www.barringtonstoke.co.uk

HarperCollins*Publishers*
Macken House, 39/40 Mayor Street Upper,
Dublin 1, DO1 C9W8, Ireland

First published in 2024

ISBN 978-1-80090-287-9

10 9 8 7 6 5 4 3 2 1

A catalogue record for this book is available from the British Library

Printed and Bound in the UK using 100% Renewable Electricity at Martins the Printers Ltd

FSC www.fsc.org MIX Paper | Supporting responsible forestry FSC™ C007454

This book contains FSC™ certified paper and other controlled sources to ensure responsible forest management.

For more information visit: www.harpercollins.co.uk/green

THE DAY OF THE JACKDAW

Jo Simmons

Illustrated by
Lee Cosgrove

Barrington Stoke

CONTENTS

CHAPTER 1

Moving

Alex was in his room. He was supposed to be tidying it. Instead, he was lying on his front, posting paperclips into a gap in the floorboards. He didn't know why he was doing that, but he enjoyed it. Then he heard his mum shouting downstairs.

"Why do we have three toasters?" she yelled.

Alex's dad shouted back to her, "It's always good to have a spare toaster. Just in case ..."

"Just in case of what?" Mum asked. "Two toasters explode at the same time? Or if they are stolen by aliens? Or eaten by racoons?"

Alex went downstairs. His mum was standing in the kitchen with one hand on her hip, staring at the three toasters on the table.

"Hey, Alex," Mum said, ruffling his hair. "I found these toasters at the back of that corner cupboard. We have collected so much stuff over the years. I suppose it's not surprising. We've lived in this house since before your sister was born."

Alex's sister, Amy, was twelve now. She was also the reason his mum was clearing out the cupboards. They were moving house. Amy had asthma, and Alex's parents had decided they should move from the city to the countryside, where the air would be cleaner.

Alex wanted to help his sister, of course he did, but he did not want to move. He had made a list of things he disliked about the countryside in his notebook called **Alex's Top-Secret Stuff**:

Too much space with no buildings

Windy

Very quiet

Weird farmyard smells even when you are not near a farmyard

Bugs

So dark at night

No friends there

Angry badgers?

Alex sat down at the table and fiddled with the dial on one of the toasters.

"Will there be angry badgers in the village we're moving to?" Alex asked.

"Not this again, Alex!" his mum sighed. "I know there were animal noises that time we went camping in the woods, and I know you thought it was angry badgers. But that was a long time ago, and I really don't think badgers get angry. Besides, we are moving to a house, not a tent, so we will be completely safe."

Alex flicked the side of one toaster with his fingernail, making a tapping sound.

"Come on, love," said his mum. "Look, I know you are worried about the move, but I think you'll love living in the countryside."

I seriously doubt that, Alex thought.

"Here, why don't you look up the village on the internet and find out more about it?" Mum said. She handed him the laptop. "It might help you feel more excited."

Alex tapped in the village name: "NOGGINGS".

What kind of a name is that for a place? Alex wondered.

Images appeared on the screen: a pretty church, a small shop, people gathered at some sort of summer fair, and lots and lots of fields.

Then Alex saw a headline from a local paper:

VILLAGE UNDER ATTACK FROM JACKDAW

What's a jackdaw? Alex wondered.

He scrolled down to find a photo of a black bird. It looked like a crow, but smaller. It had silver-grey feathers on its chest, neck and the back of its head, like it was wearing a hoodie.

Alex read the news article:

Villagers in Noggings are terrified of a local jackdaw named Graham that has been attacking them. Children were forced to play indoors after the bird dive-bombed the school playground. Graham has also targeted picnics, the local shop and dog walkers. "He's an absolute terror and a menace," one villager said. "He's a horrible, nasty thing," said another.

Alex frowned. Dangerous birds were not on his list of reasons to dislike the countryside. But they should be! Now it wasn't just angry badgers he had to watch out for, but a frightening, flapping, feathery devil called Graham.

Alex stared at the photo of Graham the jackdaw again. The bird had a thick, sharp beak and peculiar eyes. They were pale grey with black pupils. His eyes looked clever and a little bit evil, Alex thought, and a shiver skipped over his skin.

His mum peered at the screen to read the article. "That was written a week ago," she said. "That jackdaw must have flown off by now."

"I hope so," said Alex, jumping up and running for the front door.

"I'm going round to Gran's," he said.

"Ask her if she wants a toaster," Alex's mum called after him.

CHAPTER 2

Safety Cap

Alex's gran lived at the end of the road. It always took Alex exactly seventeen seconds to reach her house – unless he tripped or there was a cat or a bin in the way.

"Hey, Gran, do you need a toaster?" Alex asked when she opened the door.

"No, thanks, I already have one," she said.

"Do you want a spare? Just in case?" Alex checked.

"Just in case of what?" Gran asked.

"Never mind," said Alex.

Once inside, Alex told his gran about the jackdaw that was terrorising the village he was moving to.

"I was already nervous about moving to the countryside," Alex said. "But now there is a horrible bird picking on all the people."

"Maybe they need a brave young lad like you to save them," Gran said, smiling so that her eyes twinkled.

"Me?"

"Why not?" Gran said. "You're clever and kind, which are real superpowers, and—"

"But what about armour or weapons, Gran?" Alex said. "I will need to protect myself from this bird. He sounds really nasty."

"Have this then," Gran said. She took an old, faded baseball cap down off a peg. "Your granddad always wore this, remember? It protected him from sun, wind and rain. Perhaps it can protect you from the jackdaw."

The cap had to work. Alex's new life was about to begin in Noggings, a village under threat from a terrible, black-winged villain. He put the cap on and went to the park.

For the rest of the day, he practised defending himself against a jackdaw attack. This involved running into a group of pigeons in the park while roaring and waving a stick. It worked. The pigeons flew off in shock. Not one pecked him. Not one dive-bombed his head.

Surely the jackdaw would do the same. Graham was only a bird after all, just like these pigeons. He wasn't a threat. Perhaps he didn't even live in Noggings any more, like his mum had suggested. Or maybe Graham was no more than a village folk tale, or a rumour that had got out of hand.

Feeling much happier, Alex tossed the stick into the bushes and headed home.

CHAPTER 3

Meet the Neighbours

A few days later, Alex opened his notebook of **Top-Secret Stuff** and began a new entry:

I have lived in Noggings for three days now. I have not seen Graham the jackdaw yet, but all the local people are nervous that he might attack. When they go outside, they keep looking up at the sky. It's weird. I am wearing Granddad's cap at all times, to be safe.

At night, I hear funny animal sounds, like scratching and squeaking, coming from next door. What could be making those noises? ANGRY BADGERS?? Or Graham the jackdaw? Or is it Graham making the badgers angry? Does he pick on them too?

Alex heard a noise outside and put down his notebook. He peeped out of his window. His neighbours had pulled up, and a girl was unloading bags of straw from the back of their car. She had long brown hair tied up in a ponytail and wore a stripy T-shirt and jeans. She saw Alex and waved at him.

"Do you want to see my guinea pigs?" the girl called out.

Alex nodded and ran downstairs.

"I'm Callie by the way," she said.

"I'm Alex."

Callie led him into her house and out to the back garden. A big wire run was standing on a huge area of grass that had a wooden house at one end. Inside were ...

"Wow!" said Alex. "That's a lot of guinea pigs!"

"Twelve," said Callie.

"So that's what I've heard scuttling around and squeaking at night?" Alex asked.

"Probably," said Callie.

"Not angry badgers then?" he said.

Callie laughed and shook her head.

"And not Graham the jackdaw," Alex added.

The smile vanished from Callie's freckly face.

"Have you seen him?" Callie whispered.

"No, never. Have you?"

Callie nodded and looked serious.

"Once," she said. "I was eating an ice cream on the bench outside the village shop. Suddenly, Graham was there. He came out of nowhere. He flew *really* fast, and then he dived just like this."

Callie jabbed her hand downwards.

"Did he hurt you?" Alex asked.

"No," Callie replied. "I screamed and ran inside. But I think he took the flake from my ice cream."

"So it's food he wants?" Alex asked.

"Maybe. No one knows," Callie said. "Most of the time it's like Graham just enjoys attacking people. Like it's fun or something. What kind of a bird would do that?"

Alex shuddered and glanced up at the sky.

"Come on, let's not think about Graham any more," Callie said. She opened a door in the side of the run and scrambled inside.

Alex crawled in alongside Callie and was overrun by guinea pigs in an instant. They climbed all over him, squeaking and twitching their noses.

"It's guinea-pig world!" Alex said.

"It's guinea-pig universe!" Callie laughed.

Alex spent the rest of the day with Callie and the guinea pigs, stroking and feeding them. Maybe the countryside wasn't so bad after all, he thought. He had made one friend already – Callie. Or thirteen friends, if you counted the guinea pigs too. It made him forget all about Graham the jackdaw. Until it was time to go home for dinner.

Alex had crawled out of the pen and was brushing straw off his shorts. That was when a dark spot, moving fast in the corner of his eye, made Alex spin around.

Graham!

"Alex! Look out!" Callie shouted from inside the pen, but Alex did not move. His eyes followed the bird as it flew above him, diving and then soaring. Alex was frozen to the spot, transfixed by the sight of Graham twisting and tumbling in the sky.

Graham flew fast, changing direction in mid-air like a fighter plane. He plunged and then pulled up, wheeling around overhead. Graham got lower and closer to Alex until he made one final turn and flew fast at him. Time seemed to slow down as Alex watched Graham speeding towards him. His beak and claws were about to make contact with Alex's head, but at the last moment Graham swerved. He landed on the fence just a few steps away.

At last, Alex was face to face with the famous jackdaw. The menace that was Graham. The devilish crow-like creature that terrified everyone. Would he suddenly fly at Alex? Peck his face? Dig his black claws into his granddad's cap and rip it off?

Graham tilted his head one way then the other, staring at Alex with his bright, curious eyes. Alex could not look away from those grey eyes! Was Graham hypnotising him?

Was Graham using his eyes to send out jackdaw mindwaves and put Alex under his spell?

Then Graham was gone, as fast as he'd arrived. He took to the air with a few beats of his short black wings and flew away silently. Callie scrambled out of the pen and touched Alex's arm.

"Quick, let's get inside before Graham comes back," she gasped.

But Alex did not budge. He was breathing fast, his hands were trembling, but he felt rooted to the spot.

"Alex, come on!" Callie said. "Move!"

Graham's eyes seemed to float in front of Alex's – two silver discs. They were like evil moons with a black core. Callie tugged at Alex's arm. As if waking from a dream, he shook himself and stumbled into the house behind her.

CHAPTER 4

Time for Action!

After his brush with Graham, it took Alex an hour to pluck up the courage to run outside and back to his house.

"Where have you been?" his dad asked. "Your dinner's cold, but there's no time to eat it now. There is a meeting in the village hall tonight about that jackdaw."

"Graham?" Alex said.

"No, I'm Dad," his dad said. "My name's Pete – you know that."

"The *jackdaw* is called Graham," Alex explained.

"Yes, exactly," Dad said. "That bird dive-bombed a woman outside the shop this afternoon."

Alex gasped.

"Are you OK, Alex? You've gone pale," said his mum.

"I saw him too," Alex said in a whisper.

"The jackdaw!" screamed his mum. "Did he attack you? Are you all right?"

"I'm OK, but he scared me," Alex said. "His eyes are spooky ... And he seems smart ... It's like he's almost human ..."

Alex, his parents and Amy ran to the car, using an umbrella to protect them in case Graham attacked. When they got to the village hall, it was already full of people chattering nervously. Then a tall lady wearing a long purple dress stood up.

"Thank you all for coming," she said. "I'm Mrs Flummery, the leader of the village council. As you know, we are here to discuss the jackdaw that has been terrorising Noggings for several weeks now. He swooped down on Mrs Gertwhistle and her dog, Topsy, this afternoon. Luckily, they weren't hurt, but it can only be a matter of time before someone is injured by this avian attacker."

Someone else stood up – Mr Munch, who owned the shop. "This jackdaw is bad for my business. If he continues to target my shop, people will go elsewhere for their groceries."

"Yes, they'll go to the big supermarket in Upper Noggings," someone shouted out. "There's no deadly jackdaws there."

People murmured to agree.

"There's the summer fete in four days too," Mrs Flummery added. "We rely on the funds we raise from it to keep the playgroup open all year round. If the jackdaw attacks the fete and ruins it, the playgroup may have to close."

"We've got to do something," Mr Munch said, waving his fist. "This jackdaw menace must be taught a lesson."

People clapped.

"Graham needs to be put in his place," Mr Munch added.

People cheered.

"Stopped in his tracks," he went on.

People roared and whistled.

"Order! Order!" Mrs Flummery shouted. Everyone settled down. "Mrs Gertwhistle telephoned me before this meeting to say that

she is offering a £100 reward to anyone who can catch the jackdaw."

A ripple of excitement passed around the crowd.

"I'll catch him," someone shouted out.

"I'll stuff him too," said someone else. "He won't bother anyone then."

Some people laughed.

"Right then," said Mr Munch. "People of Noggings, this is our mission! We will catch the evil jackdaw, keep the shop safe, protect the playgroup and enjoy the best summer fete ever. The village is depending on us. Let's do this."

CHAPTER 5

The Hunt is On

The next morning, a group of local people gathered outside the shop. Alex and Callie went to watch. Some people carried big nets. Others had sticks and cages. One man had an old pillowcase with dog biscuits in the bottom that he said would act like a trap.

"I don't think jackdaws like dog biscuits," Alex whispered to Callie. "They prefer insects, fruit and seeds."

"Thank you to everyone who's joined our hunting party – and good luck!" Mr Munch called out in a big booming voice. "Go get Graham!"

The people all set off in different directions.

"Do you think they will catch him?" Callie asked Alex.

"I don't know," Alex said. "Jackdaws are expert flyers. They can twist and tumble fast. They are very intelligent birds too."

"Since when did you know so much about them?" Callie said.

"Since last night," said Alex. "I did some research about jackdaws after Graham appeared in your garden. They are also very sociable birds and tend to live in big flocks."

"But Graham's always on his own," said Callie.

"I know. It's weird, isn't it?" said Alex.

*

Later that day, Alex and Callie went back to the shop to see the hunters returning. They looked tired and sweaty. The entire village was there to meet them. Most of the hunters were empty-handed and said they hadn't even seen Graham. But then a man named Jed appeared carrying a rectangular cage covered with a pink towel.

"I got him!" Jed said. "He's in here."

A loud "quack" came from the cage.

"What was that?" Mr Munch asked.

"Nothing," said Jed.

"Let's see him then," Mr Munch said.

"He's pretty shy," Jed said. "But you can hold the cage and feel how heavy it is. Exactly the weight of a jackdaw."

“The average jackdaw weighs 220 grams,” Alex shouted out. People turned to stare at him.

“Right, let’s see,” Mr Munch said.

Suddenly, Jed looked worried and moved the cage behind him.

“Hand it over,” Mr Munch said to Jed.

Now Jed looked properly worried, but Mr Munch grabbed the cage anyway.

“That’s heavy!” Mr Munch shouted. “Far too heavy for a jackdaw weighing 220 grams. Let’s have a look.”

He whipped the towel off, and everyone gasped.

“Quack,” went the bird inside. It blinked and then ruffled its wings.

“That’s a duck, Jed, not a jackdaw,” said Mr Munch. “What were you thinking? Get lost.”

Jed slunk off.

"Don't worry, I caught him," said another man. It was Colin Featherstone, who had lived in the village since he was born. He was also carrying a cage, which was tall with a domed top. Colin lifted off the cage's red cover. Inside was a short black bird, its wrinkly grey feet gripping its perch. Alex moved forwards to get a closer look. The crowd was clapping and cheering, but Alex just stared at the bird.

"It's not Graham," Alex said, but only Callie heard him among all the roaring of the crowd.

"Are you sure?" Callie asked.

"Certain," Alex said.

"You have to say something," she said.

"No, they won't listen to me."

"Tell them," Callie said, shoving him forwards.

Alex stumbled to the front and then turned to face the crowd.

"That's not a jackdaw," Alex said.

Nobody heard him. He cleared his throat and shouted this time.

"That's not a jackdaw!"

Everyone fell silent and looked at Alex.

"Sorry," he mumbled, shrinking from all the attention.

"But it's black, with that grey head jackdaws have," said Mr Munch.

"It's the right size, isn't it?" Mrs Flummery added.

"It's Graham!" someone shouted. "I know it is!"

"Definitely Graham," someone else said. "I would know that demonic bird anywhere."

"Yes, yes, that's Graham all right," several voices called out.

"No, it isn't," said Alex. "Its eyes are golden, but a jackdaw has grey eyes. The beak is all wrong – it's too curved. That bird is heavier than a jackdaw too, and its feet aren't black like they should be – they're grey."

"Rubbish!" someone shouted.

"The boy only moved here a week or two ago – what does he know?" said Colin Featherstone, glaring at Alex.

"Now hang on," said Alex's dad, stepping forwards. "My son is allowed to say what he believes."

"Not if it's nonsense about this bird not being a jackdaw," Colin shot back.

"Are you saying my son is talking nonsense?" Alex's dad asked, sounding angry now.

"Dad, please," Alex whispered, blushing.

"I'm just saying," said Colin.

"Who's a pretty boy then?" said a voice suddenly.

The voice was loud – more of a squawk really – and it came from the bird inside the cage.

"I taught him to say that," said Colin quickly. "Jackdaws are very intelligent."

Mrs Gertwhistle leaned closer now. Her dog, Topsy, sniffed at the bird.

"Show us your knickers!" the bird squawked this time.

Mrs Gertwhistle flinched. She stared hard at the bird. After a few moments, she started to smile, then she sniggered, then she opened her mouth and laughed out loud.

"How funny!" Mrs Gertwhistle shrieked. "A talking jackdaw. I never saw anything like it!"

Then everyone else in the crowd began to laugh too.

"Show us your knickers! Show us your knickers!" squawked the bird. It bobbed up and down on its perch.

"It's a parrot," Alex said. He looked at the villagers with disbelief, but his voice was drowned out by the laughter. "The bird's feathers have been dyed black, that's all," Alex added, but no one was listening, not even Callie.

"The deadly jackdaw has been caught and is no longer a threat!" Mr Munch roared, beaming a big smile at everyone. "But he is a bit cheeky!

Dear me! To think this funny little bird had us all shaking in our boots. Well, never mind. It looks as if the village fete can go ahead as planned this Sunday."

"And congratulations to Mr Colin Featherstone," Mrs Gertwhistle said. She handed him an envelope stuffed with prize money.

Everyone cheered. Alex slipped away from the crowd and walked home. The only one who saw him leave was a small black bird with cool grey eyes, sitting on the roof of the shop.

CHAPTER 6

A Fete Worse than Death

The day of the Noggings summer fete arrived. There had been no sightings of Graham since Colin Featherstone had "caught" him four days before. Everyone in the village was sure that the dark threat of a jackdaw attack was gone. Everyone apart from Alex.

People were in a festive mood. They were excited to enjoy the annual village celebration and fundraiser, free from jackdaw jitters.

The fete was taking place inside the village hall and its big garden. There were stalls selling plants, books and homemade jam. There was a Best Victoria Sponge competition, with all the cakes lined up waiting to be judged. There were prized vegetables on show too, including Noggings' Biggest Onion.

Outside, there was a van cooking burgers, a bouncy castle and some games including Guess How Many Sweets in a Jar, a coconut shy and skittles.

Alex's gran had come to visit so she could see the fete. While she went off to inspect the giant tomatoes, Alex went to find Callie, who was running the petting zoo.

"Is it just guinea pigs in the zoo?" Alex asked. He recognised Parsnip, Coco and Ralph in the little pen.

"So far," said Callie, "but Mr Munch is bringing his pet slug."

"Maybe Colin Featherstone will bring that bird he says is Graham," Alex added.

Callie frowned at him. “Don’t go on about that any more, Alex. Everyone believes that bird was the jackdaw. Maybe it was.”

“It wasn’t,” Alex muttered.

“So what?” Callie said. “Everyone is happy and relieved and wants to have a good day at the fete. Can’t you too?”

“OK, OK,” Alex said, but he couldn’t help glancing up at the sky. “Can I stroke one of your guinea pigs, please?”

“That costs 50p,” Callie said.

“50p!” Alex yelped. “It’s free when I stroke them at your house.”

“We are raising money for the playgroup, remember?” Callie said.

Alex tutted and handed over a 50p coin, then sat down and cuddled Parsnip in his lap.

He watched all the villagers enjoying the fete and began to relax. So maybe Colin Featherstone had not caught Graham, but perhaps the hunt had scared the jackdaw away. Maybe Graham had realised he wasn't wanted here and had flown off to live somewhere else. And even if Graham was still around, surely he wouldn't dare attack such a large, crowded event?

Then Alex heard a scream and felt Parsnip freeze in his lap. Parsnip knew, with her guinea-pig instinct, that danger had arrived at the Noggings summer fete.

Another scream now pierced the air! And another!

Alex jumped up and quickly put Parsnip back in her cage. He turned to see the villagers running in all directions with their hands over their heads. Above them was a bird darting down into the crowd and then soaring back up. It was a jackdaw.

"Graham," Alex said, and a shiver ran down his spine.

"Run!" Callie shouted, and sprinted away.

People were rushing back to the safety of the hall, some of them hiding under picnic tables before dashing forwards. But Alex carried on watching Graham.

The beady-eyed bird swooped at the bunting and used his beak to rip it down. Then he scattered the skittles, shredded the sandwiches

and wrecked the raffle. With one mighty swoop, he knocked over the How Many Sweets in a Jar, sending its contents tumbling away while he made a cry that sounded like "Tchack! Tchack!"

Next, Graham grabbed a half-eaten burger, flew up high with it and dropped it on Mr Munch's head. He swooped down again and popped a child's balloon with his beak. Then he landed for a few seconds on the bouncy castle, pecking a tiny hole in one of its turrets so that air started to whoosh out.

Graham had transformed a happy summer fete into a scene of chaos, with people tripping up and tumbling as they tried to escape. A child wailed and pointed at their teddy, dropped in the grass and now being trampled by the stampede of people.

Mr Munch screamed, "Get inside! Save yourselves! Run!"

But Alex heard a different cry.

"Topsy! Topsy! Where are you?"

It was Mrs Gertwhistle, who was still outside. She would not leave her beloved Topsy, but where was the dog?

Alex scanned the garden and spotted the small white dog trembling under a bush at the far end. He ran, weaving his way between the remaining people racing in the opposite direction. Alex leaped over a mess of scattered chips, swerved around an upturned picnic table and rushed past the burger van. He then ran the final few metres towards the bush where Topsy was hiding.

Alex had nowhere to hide, and there were no other people this far down the garden. He was a clear target as he clasped Topsy to his chest and sped back towards the hall.

"Don't look behind you!" Callie shouted. She was standing in the doorway of the village hall with Mrs Gertwhistle, beckoning Alex inside. "Keep running!"

Alex could sense Graham was getting closer. He even thought he could hear his wings beating just behind him, but he didn't look back. Alex kept running and, with a final blast of energy, leaped inside the hall.

Callie slammed the door shut, and Alex fell to the floor, panting. Topsy gave a whimper and then licked Alex's face. They were safe – for now.

CHAPTER 7

Fight Back

It was quiet in the hall. People sat in groups, hugging each other and checking their injuries. Mr Munch had sprained his ankle as he'd rushed to safety. One small child had got candy floss stuck in his ear, and another was hiccupping with fright.

"We need to go back out there and fight Graham," said Mr Munch. "I can't because of my ankle, but *somebody* does."

"That's right. We can't stay trapped in here because of a bird," said Alex's dad. "I'll go."

"Me too," said Mrs Flummery.

"And what about you?" said Mrs Gertwhistle. She pointed at Colin Featherstone, who was holding his birdcage. "That bird that you claimed was Graham is clearly *not* Graham. The least you can do is go outside and tackle the real Graham."

Topsy the dog yipped to agree.

"We will need protective clothing," said Alex's dad. "Is there anything in the hall we can use?"

"Only the playgroup's dressing-up clothes," said Mrs Flummery.

The three volunteers searched inside the box of dressing-up clothes and selected their armour. Alex's dad wore a yellow plastic fireman's helmet that was so small it sat on the top of his head like a cherry on a cake. Mrs Flummery chose a red Superman cape and carried a Victoria sponge cake. She explained that she was hoping to throw it at Graham, to knock him out of the sky with a giant splat of sponge, jam and buttercream. Colin Featherstone picked a green plastic lightsaber as his weapon.

"Ready?" asked Callie, standing at the door.

"Ready," said Alex's dad.

Callie pulled back the bolt and threw the door open.

The small army advanced into the garden and stopped in the middle. Where was Graham?

They stood back to back for several minutes until Alex's dad shrugged and wandered back towards the hall.

"He's not here," he said to all the villagers who were huddled by the windows watching nervously. "I reckon it's probably safe to—"

WHAM!

Graham swooped at Alex's dad from behind, knocking the fireman's helmet off his head. He swooped again, aiming at Mrs Flummery this time. She shrieked and flung the Victoria sponge up into the air, completely missing Graham, who was now preparing to dive-bomb Colin Featherstone.

Rather than raise his lightsaber and brace for the attack, Colin waved it around his head wildly with his eyes closed. "Get away from me!" he shouted. "Get away!"

"Pull back!" Callie yelled to the warriors from the open hall door. "Retreat! Retreat!"

Colin Featherstone shot inside first. Then Alex's dad hooked his arm into Mrs Flummery's and together they staggered into the hall. Callie slammed the door behind them.

"What now?" said Mr Munch.

"We're trapped, aren't we?" said Mrs Gertwhistle. Topsy whimpered and began to shake again.

"Terrifying," muttered Mrs Flummery. "That bird is completely terrifying."

"There's no taming that thing. He's out of control," Alex's dad said, wiping sweat from his forehead with his sleeve.

"Let me try," said Alex.

"What?" said several people.

"No way, son," said Alex's dad. "It's too dangerous."

"Please. I want to," Alex said.

The hall became utterly silent as everyone stared at Alex. Then his gran stepped forwards, and with a warm smile, she nodded. Alex nodded back and moved towards the door.

"I can't let you go out there," Alex's mum said, grabbing his arm with tears in her eyes.

"It's OK, Mum," Alex said. "I'm wearing Granddad's lucky cap." He touched it and smiled.

"Take this too," said Colin, handing him the plastic lightsaber.

"And this," said Mrs Flummery, tying the red cape around Alex.

"Who's a pretty boy then?" said the parrot.

"Callie – open the door," Alex said.

Again, Callie slid back the bolt.

"Good luck," she said. Callie touched Alex on the arm quickly, and then she swung the door open.

CHAPTER 8

A Boy and a Bird

Alex walked out into the garden. He could sense the villagers staring at him, their faces pressed up to the hall windows. He moved slowly, watching the sky and scanning the trees.

His toe tapped against something on the grass, and he looked down. It was the yellow plastic fireman's helmet. Next to it were a few scattered chips and some of the Victoria sponge, which had exploded into lots of cakey pieces as soon as it hit the ground.

Alex waited. He was aware that his heart was beating faster than normal, but his hands were not shaking, and he didn't move.

It seemed like hours had passed when Graham finally appeared, but it had really only been about three minutes. At first, he looked like an empty black crisp packet, blowing in the wind, swinging this way and that. But as he got nearer, Alex could make out Graham's curved wings and neat, blunt tail. Then he did a final twist in the air and began to dive.

Alex could hear the people in the hall shriek, but he stood still and did not duck as Graham sped towards him. He felt a blast of air as the bird whooshed past, millimetres away from his face. It made him stagger backwards.

"I'm OK!" Alex shouted, glancing back at the people in the hall.

He touched the brim of his cap lightly, glad to have it on his head. Gran had said the cap had protected his granddad from all sorts of danger. Then Alex remembered that she had said other things too, about Alex having real superpowers ...

Alex looked up. Graham was wheeling around in the sky above him again, preparing to dive for a second time. Rather than brace himself, Alex yanked at the strings of the cape and pulled it off. Then he tossed the lightsaber away. Last of all, he took off his cap and put it carefully on the picnic table next to him.

Graham flew closer.

"I am not armed," Alex shouted up at the bird, his arms spread wide.

Graham swooped rapidly, as if he was taking a closer look at the boy standing in shorts and a T-shirt, with no weapons and not even his lucky cap.

"I mean you no harm," Alex called. "I am not a threat. Can't we have peace?"

Graham flapped past him, his loud "Tchack, tchack" call sounding extra cross.

"Come on, Graham, let's talk about this," Alex called out. His eyes tracked the bird as it swerved above him. "Graham! Please!"

Was the bird listening? Alex didn't know. All he could see was Graham flip in the air and dive back towards him.

"He's swooping right at Alex!" Mrs Gertwhistle shrieked.

"He's aiming for his head," said Mr Munch.

"I can't watch," gasped Mrs Flummery.

"Give us a kiss," said the parrot.

But Alex was not afraid. He fixed his eyes on Graham, watching him swerve and tilt, closer and closer. He realised that Graham was not aiming for Alex's head but for the picnic table. He spread his wings to act like brakes, paused in the air and then landed softly on it. Graham peered at Alex, his head on one side.

"What on earth is the boy doing now?" Mr Munch asked, watching from the window.

"I think he's talking to the bird," Alex's mum said.

Mr Munch shook his head. "He needs to catch it, not have a chat with it."

But Alex wasn't planning to catch Graham. In fact, he had put some chips on his palm, and Graham had hopped over. After staring at them for a few seconds, Graham suddenly hopped onto Alex's hand and began pecking up the chips. His pointed beak tapped against Alex's skin painlessly and made him laugh out loud.

"Alex is feeding him now!" Mr Munch shrieked.

"Be quiet, Mr Munch," Mrs Flummery snapped back. "Let the boy do his work."

The villagers were gripped. They could not look away and didn't notice Callie slipping out of the hall to join Alex.

"How did you do that?" Callie asked once she was alongside Alex. "He's eating out of your hand!"

"Isn't it great?" Alex said, giggling.

"But how did you dare? He could have hurt you."

"Remember I found out that jackdaws tend to gather in flocks, but Graham was always on his own?"

"Yes," said Callie.

"Well, I know what it's like to turn up in a new village and not know anyone and feel like you don't belong. You need a friend. I had you, but who does Graham have?"

"So he's lonely, is that it?" Callie asked.

"Maybe," Alex said.

"But why would he attack everyone?"

"He never actually attacked anyone, did he?" Alex said. "Graham dive-bombed, but he never pecked or scratched. He always pulled away before that. It was all of us that decided he was dangerous."

Callie frowned.

"Let's give him a chance," Alex said.

He put a chip on his shoulder, and Graham hopped up to eat it.

Callie darted backwards. "Careful, Alex! He's right by your ear."

But Graham just pecked softly at Alex's hair, combing it with his beak.

Alex laughed, but inside the hall, everyone gasped. He turned slowly, with Graham still on his shoulder. Alex smiled at all the faces peering out of the hall windows, then gave them a thumbs up.

Slowly, the people inside seemed to understand.

Their faces shifted from expressions of shock to delight. They smiled and nodded and then gave a huge cheer.

Alex laughed, and Graham flew up and did a few acrobatic loops in the air. This time he landed on Callie's shoulder. She cringed a bit, but Alex's big smile reassured her, and she soon began to laugh.

"Graham, you're the best," Callie whispered, stroking the grey feathers of his chest with one finger.

The villagers cheered some more.

Alex stood close to Graham and whispered to him. "Now, if I get everyone outside, do you promise not to attack them?"

Graham looked at Alex with his bright eyes, then seemed to bob his head.

"I'll take that as a yes," Alex said.

CHAPTER 9

A Warm Welcome

Of course Graham couldn't resist dive-bombing a few of the villagers once they were all gathered outside to properly meet him. But Alex reassured them that he meant no harm, and slowly everyone relaxed.

"He's a lively little fellow," said Mrs Flummery, looking half curious and half nervous.

"Polly seems to like him," said Colin Featherstone. The parrot was bobbing about in her cage and beating her wings. This had rubbed some of the black dye off her feathers, revealing their true green colour.

"We should let the local paper know," said Mr Munch. "I'm sure they'll be interested in how we have made friends with our foe."

"Perhaps Graham could become the village animal?" Alex suggested. "Graham the menace becomes Graham the mascot?"

"What a lovely idea," said Mrs Gertwhistle. "And, Colin Featherstone, you can give that reward for catching Graham to Alex."

"Oh," said Colin, like a sulky child. "I've already spent some of it on new roller skates."

"I don't care," said Mrs Gertwhistle firmly. "You owe Alex £100. Really it should be a great deal more. He didn't just catch that little flapping firebrand – Alex understood him, and now Graham can become a valued member of our village. That feels priceless."

Alex smiled. His gran came over.

"I knew your superpowers would save the day," she whispered into his ear. "Cleverness and kindness. Well done, Alex. You didn't need your granddad's cap after all."

"Thanks, Gran," said Alex. He hugged her, but their cuddle was interrupted by Mr Munch shouting, "Welcome to the village, Graham!"

There was more cheering, and Graham flapped around a bit, clacking his beak and saying, "Tchack, tchack".

"And welcome to the village, Alex. We are delighted to have you living in Noggings," Mr Munch said. "Now, to celebrate, how about some Victoria sponge and a giant tomato?"

Everyone cheered.

CHAPTER 10

Final Thoughts

Alex's Top-Secret Stuff:

True facts I have learned so far since moving to Noggings:

Graham the jackdaw is not at all scary – he's brilliant.

The countryside is not at all scary either – there are no angry badgers!

A black parrot is not a jackdaw. It's just a parrot with dodgy dyed feathers!

Also ...

There were a lot of sweets in that jar that Graham knocked over. It took me, Callie, Mum, Dad and Amy ages to pick them all up. We didn't count them, but I did get to keep them. WIN!

I also got the £100 for helping Graham make friends with all of us. EXTRA WIN!

I will spend some on bird food. Not the usual kind. Graham likes spaghetti hoops! And I will spend some on a new home for Callie's guinea pigs in my garden. I am going to call it the Guinea Crib. We are building a tunnel under the fence so they can live on both sides.

Amy hasn't had a single asthma attack since we moved here. So it looks like we are staying. That's fine by me (surprised face!)

I've got to go. Graham is outside. I have promised to make him a nest in the tree outside, using Granddad's old cap and some guinea-pig straw.

Chill out, Graham, I'm coming! Keep your feathers on!

Our books are tested for children and young people by children and young people.

Thanks to everyone who consulted on a manuscript for their time and effort in helping us to make our books better for our readers.